For Roger and Amy, S.G.

First published in 1997
by Macdonald Young Books
an imprint of Wayland publishers Ltd
61 Western Road
Hove
East Sussex
BN3 1JD

Typeset in Bembo 20pt by Goodfellow and Egan Ltd, Cambridge
Printed and bound in Belgium by Proost International Book Production

British Library Cataloguing in Publication Data available.

ISBN: 0 7500 2018 0
ISBN: 0 7500 2019 9 (pb)

SALLY GRINDLEY

There's a monster who eats books in our house

Illustrated by Arthur Robins

MACDONALD YOUNG BOOKS